Our friends in chairs with wheels

Carrie L. Case
&
Faith Ecklund

tate publishing
CHILDREN'S DIVISION

Published by Tate Publishing & Enterprises, LLC
127 E. Trade Center Terrace | Mustang, Oklahoma 73064 USA
1.888.361.9473 | www.tatepublishing.com

Tate Publishing is committed to excellence in the publishing industry. The company reflects the philosophy established by the founders, based on Psalm 68:11,
"The Lord gave the word and great was the company of those who published it."

Published in the United States of America

ISBN: 978-1-62854-396-4
1. Juvenile Nonfiction / Social Issues / Special Needs
2. Juvenile Nonfiction / Poetry / General
14.05.27

FREE music download of the song
"That's How We Roll," by Faith Ecklund
with book purchase.

Scan this:

or visit www.faithecklundmusic.com
to get your FREE download.

Also available for purchase, Faith Ecklund's new EP
"I Wanna Walk With You."

DEDICATION

To Dad...creative, fun, witty, intelligent, kind, giving, loved, missed. You weren't just her shining star; you were mine too. To Adelynne, Eleanor, and Lilyanna: Mommy and Auntie Faith love you!

—Carrie L. Case

Shane, it's because of you I have done things I never thought I could. You have encouraged me to become comfortable enough in my own skin to share my story with others. Thank you for always loving and being supportive in all the dreams I dare to dream. I love you!

—Faith Ecklund

FORWARD

This book is a result of growing up with a father in a wheelchair and observing the sometimes-odd reactions shown towards him. Seeing someone in a wheelchair was often foreign to others but normal to our family. Their reactions resonate in my memory and my heart. When my dad passed away while I was pregnant with my first child, his first grandchild, I wanted to be sure my kids treated everyone the same, that they would not react to a wheelchair with surprise, discomfort, or fear. Growing up with Auntie Faith in their lives certainly brings normalcy to knowing someone who uses a wheelchair, but not everyone has a Daddy Jer or an Auntie Faith. This is our cooperative way of showing children (and parents too) that people in wheelchairs are just people. It is just another person's normal.

We love our friends for who they are.
They may not look like you and me,

but we love them always
even if they have a
disability.

Be curious, ask questions, but there's no need to stare.
The only real difference is they use a wheelchair.

Our friends may have gotten a big
giant boo-boo!
Sometimes this happens to little
puppies too.

Sometimes they get sick and can't walk like they did in the past,

So with the help of their
wheelchair they can go super fast!

Our friends are tall and small,
young and old.

They have long hair like a lion

and bald heads that get cold.

They have blue eyes and brown eyes
and green ones too.

Our friends do a lot of the same things that you and I do.

They ride bikes

and draw cartoons,

go to work in a car.

They go to school to
learn math,

and they play the guitar.

They cook...

and they garden.

They go
shopping for
shoes.

Our friends sing pretty songs

and silly songs too.

They play puzzles with pieces and puzzles with words.

They have hobbies like fishing

and looking
at birds.

They watch
game shows,

play on the
beach,

and surf
the web.

They scrapbook,

take baths,

and take naps in their beds.

Even though we all are different there's no need to stare.
Treat everyone the same. Say "Hello!" Help and share.

Treat everyone equally, always be kind and care. God loves us all, whether we walk or use a wheelchair.

Symbol Search

The handicap sign is used to help our friends in chairs with wheels. You'll find it in parking lots, near doors, in bathrooms and more! Go back through the book and count how many you see. There are 22 hidden throughout the book (don't forget the cover)! Visit *www.friendsinchairswithwheels.com* to find out where. You'll also be able to meet the Our Friends gang and do other cool stuff.

 Carrie L. Case grew up with her father in a wheelchair. The way people would react to her dad inspired Carrie to write a book for children (and parents) about how to treat people with disabilities. Carrie is a Graphic Designer by trade and resides in Fircrest, Washington with her husband Chris, three daughters, and her dog, Buddy.

 In 1997, Faith Ecklund was in a car accident that left her paralyzed. For some, seeing her in a chair is strange, but to her, it has become her normal. Faith's hope for the book is that it will encourage others to ask questions, and become more comfortable with seeing people in wheelchairs. Faith lives in Nashville, Tennessee with her husband, Shane, and two dogs, Berkeley and Ellie Mae.

listen|imagine|view|experience

AUDIO BOOK DOWNLOAD INCLUDED WITH THIS BOOK!

In your hands you hold a complete digital entertainment package. In addition to the paper version, you receive a free download of the audio version of this book. Simply use the code listed below when visiting our website. Once downloaded to your computer, you can listen to the book through your computer's speakers, burn it to an audio CD or save the file to your portable music device (such as Apple's popular iPod) and listen on the go!

How to get your free audio book digital download:

1. Visit www.tatepublishing.com and click on the e|LIVE logo on the home page.
2. Enter the following coupon code:
   dc33-a3c2-9557-2142-e7e4-837a-3240-9dbd
3. Download the audio book from your e|LIVE digital locker and begin enjoying your new digital entertainment package today!